To ou[r]

in F[

C.N.K (Y*ϕ*N)

MW00911003

My Christmas Secret

Christopher Kringle

Illustrated by Gennel Marie Sollano

To order additional copies of this book, contact:
Xlibris
1-888-795-4274
www.Xlibris.com
Orders@Xlibris.com

ISBN: Softcover   978-1-7960-6227-4
      Hardcover   978-1-7960-6228-1
      EBook   978-1-7960-6226-7

Print information available on the last page

Rev. date: 09/25/2019

My Christmas Secret

They deserve all the credit.
Many miles they fly
without a complaint
they never ask why.

No team of horses
no creatures so grand
as these wonderful reindeer
who are at my command.

Dancer and Dasher
are next in the traces.
Dancer, is graceful
and Dasher, he races.

And when Christmas comes
at the end of the year
like magic the presents
just seem to appear.

The joy that we get from the gifts that we give helps us stay young and continue to live.

The face of a person on Christmas morning when they open a present is really quite warming.

For a world that we love
to toil's a pleasure.
It gives each of us
a true Christmas Treasure.

A simple rule
by which we live.
It's not what you get;
it's what you give.

Christopher N. Kringle

Printed in the United States
By Bookmasters